BLURRED REALITY

EVAN JACOBS

D1021653

SADDLEBACK
EDUCATIONAL PUBLISHING

MONARCH JUNGLE

SADDLEBACK
EDUCATIONAL PUBLISHING
www.sdlback.com

Copyright ©2018 by Saddleback Educational Publishing
All rights reserved. No part of this book may be reproduced in any form or by any means, electronic or mechanical, including photocopying, recording, scanning, or by any information storage and retrieval system, without the written permission of the publisher. SADDLEBACK EDUCATIONAL PUBLISHING and any associated logos are trademarks and/or registered trademarks of Saddleback Educational Publishing.

ISBN-13: 978-1-68021-479-6
ISBN-10: 1-68021-479-9
eBook: 978-1-63078-833-9

Printed in Guangzhou, China
NOR/1117/CA21701345

22 21 20 19 18   1 2 3 4 5

MONARCH
JUNGLE

Chapter 1

Killing It

Yeah!" Alden shouted. He sat at a computer. Fingers of one hand tapped the keyboard. The other hand moved the mouse. His eyes darted around the screen.

A young woman sat next to him. "No!" she shouted back.

They were talking to each other through headsets.

"Bad move," Alden said.

"Dude!" she said. "Are you kidding me?"

"You shouldn't be alive!" he said.

The players were tense. There was a lot to gain. And even more to lose. Reputation. Money. Pride. This was the world of eSports. It was as big as pro football.

Alden went pro a year ago. He was a PC player. Many gamers would laugh at that. They only used consoles.

In the gaming world, it was a big debate. For Alden, it was about click speed. The PC was faster. The mouse gave good aim. That mattered in shooting games. Consoles gathered dust.

But Alden didn't make excuses. He won. His gamer name was "Black Heart." And he was in the world's top 10.

Today's game was *Dead End*. There was violence, of course. Guns. Lasers or bombs. Fist fighting at times.

Each level had two tasks. Kill the enemy and escape. There were only minutes. It took quick decisions. Fail, and your avatar died.

Alden was facing a great player. Her name was Kady Adams. "Red Ivy" was her gamer name. No one had played *Dead End* better. That would change today. It was Alden's hope anyway.

Now the two sat side by side. People looking down saw only two small dots. That didn't matter. The arena was filled with big screens. That's where the action was seen.

Black Heart was a pirate. He had long brown hair. Red Ivy's hair was crimson. She was dressed in a tank top and fatigues.

They fought. Guns went off. There were explosions. People watched in awe.

Every attack got cheers. Alden didn't hear them. His headset blocked the sound. For now, the real world didn't exist. He was in the zone.

There were five rounds altogether. So far, Alden had won two. He needed one more win. Then he would sweep the series. But Kady had never lost this game.

Today was different. Alden was feeling bold. He'd even said it to reporters. "Red Ivy is going down."

The third round started. It was set in a chemical plant. A fire was raging. They had one minute to work it out.

"I'm coming for you," Alden said into his headset. "That's right. Stay right there."

"Get off my back!" Kady yelled.

Bullets flew past Black Heart. They hit a tank of gas. Flames shot up. More tanks burst open. There was a string of explosions.

"Oh my God," Alden said.

Black Heart flew across the room. He was down. Red Ivy started shooting.

Nine, ten, eleven. Alden was counting to himself. He knew her gun had twelve bullets. One more bullet and she'd have to reload. *Twelve.*

Suddenly Black Heart stood. The crowd gasped. This was sure death. Red Ivy's gun clicked. She reached for another one. In that second, she was shot.

"Got you!" Alden shouted. The screens went black. The crowd roared. He jumped to his feet.

"Nicely done," Kady said.

The two shook hands. Then the crowd rushed in around him.

"You're the greatest gamer in the world," someone shouted.

"Nah," Alden said. He didn't like to brag. It was better to act humble. "But I did kill it today."

Chapter 2

FEELING THE LOVE

Alden was having dinner with his parents. They were at a restaurant. His girlfriend, Lia, was there too. The meal was his treat.

"Here's to my son." Alden's dad lifted his glass. "I'd like to take credit. But I can't," he said. "I don't know a joystick from a stick of gum."

Everyone at the table laughed. They raised their water glasses. "Cheers!"

His mom smiled. "Thank you for being so good at what you do."

"Gee, thanks, Mom."

"There's one thing I don't understand," she said. "Why does your name have to be Black Heart? You're such a nice young man."

Everyone laughed again. Alden just smiled.

Gamers as good as Alden made big money. He often spent it on the people he loved. It made him happy. The times they were together meant a lot. But that didn't stop him from texting at the table.

"Who is it, Alden?" Lia asked. "Can't it wait?"

"It's just some gamer friends. They're stoked about my win. I'll be off in a sec."

She looked at his phone. "Wait. What's this? You're playing a video game?" She looked up at Alden's parents. "It's *Duck Shoot*. The lamest game ever."

Lia didn't treat Alden like a star. She didn't care about him being a big gamer. Or that he'd gotten rich off it. She liked him because he was funny. When he acted like a jerk, she called him on it. Alden liked that about her.

"Stop hating," Alden said. "You know I love this game."

"He can't help himself," his dad said. "And we don't want him to. Keep playing, son."

"Right," Alden said. "Video games are paying for dinner!"

Alden's mom and dad laughed. Lia gave him a nudge. He was the center of attention. That's the way he liked it.

After dinner, Alden walked Lia to her car. "Did you have fun?" he asked.

She nodded. He pulled her in and hugged her. She

always smelled so good. Tonight she smelled like coconut. He kissed her.

"I'll text you later," he said.

She got into her car and drove off. Alden looked at his phone. His agent had texted him during dinner.

"Call me ASAP. Great news."

Alden decided to call in the morning. Business could wait.

Chapter 3

Nothing to Lose

It was the next day after school. Alden was waiting for Lia.

"Hey, Alden," a voice called. "I saw you play *Dead End*. That was a sick kill."

"Thanks, bro!" Alden didn't know the kid. But most students at Volt High knew Alden. He got a lot of respect. Even the teachers loved him.

Alden's phone buzzed. It was Zac Elliot. He was the best agent in gaming. All the good talent went with Zac. Alden hired him a year ago. There had been many big deals since then.

"Hey, Zac. What's up?"

"Great news," Zac said. "Your last win got a lot of hype. Some big gaming execs saw it. They want you to play for them. It's a VR game."

"Oh man, Zac. Not virtual reality. You know how—"

"Before you say anything, just listen. This is different."

"There's no way. I'm not wearing one of those headsets. They're heavy. I sweat like a pig. And I hate using a controller."

"This is new technology."

"I've heard that before," Alden said.

"I have two words for you. *World Quest*. They're testing it. This is a contest. Does that change your mind?"

"Maybe," Alden said. "Tell me more."

World Quest was made by Grunt Games. All the best games came from them. *Warped. Click. Chaos.* It was because of the man who made them. Andrew Foster.

His games didn't seem like games. The images were real. And the stories had meaning. Every game had tons of hidden secrets. There was real-time action. Players didn't wait for a turn. It was a total experience. So yeah. If anyone could make VR better, it was Foster. Some called him a mastermind.

Alden had heard how the game worked. A friend of his was in the business. She was a coder. *World Quest* used a headset. It read a player's brain. They just had to think their actions.

It sounded good. But it hadn't been proven. And the game itself seemed kind of lame. In fairness, many did on paper.

The task was to save Earth. A deadly disease was killing off the planet. There was a cure. It came in eight hidden bottles. Each avatar was dropped in a random place. It could be anywhere in the universe. They each had four lives.

"Who am I up against?" Alden asked.

"The best. Nina Lenz from Germany. Lee Yang from China. Dev Reddy from India."

"Okay," Alden said. Dev's name was a surprise. Players from Russia or Korea were always among the top. But eSports had gotten so big. And the names were always changing.

"I'm still listening." Knowing Zac, it had to be a sweet deal.

"Players will be in their own countries. You'll be at Grunt Games. Millions will watch over the internet. The game will last four hours."

"That's a long day. What's the top prize?"

"One million dollars. Fourth place is 100 thousand. You can't lose. So are you in?"

Alden was quiet. He liked to tease Zac. "Heck yeah!" he finally said.

Chapter 4

Psyched

Alden hadn't seen Lia come up beside him.

"You look excited. What's going on?" she asked.

"Oh, not much. Just a million bucks."

"Let me guess. For playing a video game. Must be nice."

"Do you want to hear about it?"

"Sure. You can tell me at the mall. Remember? We have a date?"

"Right," he said.

It was their favorite thing to do. They'd walk around for a while. Have some coffee. Then they would sit and watch people. Make up stories about them. It was always good for a laugh.

Alden liked hanging out with Lia. She wasn't into

gaming at all. It was his chance to disconnect from it. He'd even stay off his phone. He would try to anyway.

But not today. The *World Quest* contest was in a few days. That was all he could think about.

"I'll meet you there after school," he said to Lia. "I just want to get a little gaming in first."

Lia rolled her eyes and walked away.

It was five o'clock. Alden had finally made it to the mall. He found Lia inside the food court. The first thing he did was check his phone. His knee bounced nervously up and down.

"So much for being together. Can't you think about something else? Like me?" Lia said.

"Look, babe," Alden said. "We need to enjoy all this while it lasts."

"Enjoy all what? You glued to your phone?"

"There has to be a game I can't win. *World Quest* could be the one. And then all the money and fame will be gone."

"Someone beat the great Alden Nash? Not likely."

"VR isn't my game of choice. So I'll probably suck at it. But there is one good thing."

Lia smiled. "So it's not just about the money."

Alden looked a little surprised. "Ouch," he said in a

playful voice. "How can you even say that? You know how much I love gaming. Besides, I'll get to meet a genius."

Andrew Foster was never seen in public. He didn't do interviews. There were no photos of him online. Meeting him was a big deal.

GRUNT GAMES

Alden had a car take him to Grunt Games. Four hours was a long time to play. He knew he'd be fried. This way he didn't have to worry about driving.

The building wasn't fancy. It was a tall gray block of concrete. There were no signs. No company logo. No windows. It was the same inside. Gray, plain, and cold.

"Hello, Alden," a woman said. "I'm Lana Wong. I'll take you to the player room. First you have to pass security."

This was normal for big gaming companies. They all had tight security. There were so many threats. It could be cyberattacks or scammers. Games could be leaked. Even ideas got stolen.

Lana led him to a metal detector. A guard collected his phone and keys.

"You really think I'm a risk? Look at me," Alden said. "I'm puny."

The guard gave him a cold look.

Alden walked through the scanner. He was clean.

"This way," Lana said.

"What about my phone and—"

"You'll get them back at the end. Follow me."

She led him into a large room. There was a table and a chair. On the table was a headset. One wall was all mirror. *People must be behind it watching*, Alden thought.

A man's voice came over a speaker. "Hello, Mr. Nash. Please have a seat."

Alden sat down.

"Are you ready to begin?"

"Sure." He gave a wave toward the mirror.

Lana stepped up to Alden. She was pressing something onto his head.

"What's this?" Alden asked.

"Sensors," the voice said. "They will let you feel things like heat."

"No one told me about it."

Lana put sensors on his arms and legs too. From under the table, she brought up a keyboard and mouse.

"What's this for?" Alden asked. "I thought this game uses brainwaves."

"It's only if you need it," the voice said. "We want you to be comfortable. Now put on the headset. Make sure it fits well. Let us know if you need help."

"Is this Andrew Foster?" Alden asked. He was only half joking.

There was no answer. *Geez, people. Lighten up.* Was this a game? Or was he on trial? *Remember who you are,* he thought. *You live for pressure.*

Alden put on the headset. All he saw was darkness.

"Feel okay?" the voice asked.

"Yeah. It's light. Just like the reviews said. I'm surprised."

"You're a bit of a wise guy. I like that. Now let's begin. Please press the start button. It's on the right side of your headset."

Alden reached up. He pressed the button.

"You should see a large screen," the voice said. "It's split into four panels. There is one for each player. This is what people watching online will see."

Alden looked at his panel. It showed a picture of his avatar. He'd changed his look since the *Dead End* win.

Instead of long hair, he had a Mohawk. His muscles were bigger. Battle scars covered his bare arms. Guns and bullets were strapped to his vest. A large blade was at his side.

He noticed the other panels. Nina's avatar, Cosma, had pink hair. She wore a blue leather jumpsuit.

Lee was Mad Dog. He wore a dark suit. His head was mostly shaved. And he had long bleached bangs.

Dev was Destroyer. He was a warrior dressed in armor.

"You can check scores any time. Tap the side of your headset. Or just say the word *score*. Note that the time is 11:02. Begin," the voice said.

Rush

Alden's body was gone. But he had his thoughts. And he could sense everything. Black Heart stood in a war zone. The details of the scene were sharp.

Bombs went off. Cars crashed and burned. People fought in the streets. Most buildings were on fire. The others had been broken into. The entire city was wrecked.

Alden felt the heat from the fires. How was this happening? Oh yeah. The sensors. Pieces of debris flew in Black Heart's face. He started to run, his arms pumping. But there was nowhere to go.

"Whoa!" Alden had played many VR games. But they were nothing like this. The hype was right. *World Quest* was as real as it got.

Stay calm, he told himself. That's what pros did. They were fearless. And they didn't quit. Alden would do what it took to win. That's when he remembered the goal of the game. Find the cure.

At that moment there was a screeching noise. A truck came speeding around the corner. It was rolling over cars and people. Black Heart stood in its path.

This called for a split decision. Get out of the way or go for it. It was the last second. *Jump*, Alden thought. Black Heart stepped off with one foot. He leaped onto the hood of the truck.

What a rush! This was VR on steroids!

He could see the driver through the windshield. It was Cosma. She sped up. Black Heart moved forward. He punched the windshield. The glass cracked and shattered. As she took out her gun, he dived inside.

He grabbed her. They started to wrestle. She pulled the trigger. Alden felt a burning pain go through his body. She'd shot Black Heart. He put a hand to his head. He could feel the warm blood.

Cosma smiled. Then her eyes got wide. Black Heart turned his head to look. The road ended up ahead. It looked like it just stopped. Beyond that was sky.

They flew over the edge. The truck was in a nose-dive. Directly below was ocean. There was no way they'd survive this.

Cosma may have taken Black Heart's life. But he was taking her down too.

Alden tapped his headset. He read the score.

"Lives used: 1. Lives left: 3."

Then everything went black.

GASP

Black Heart lay on the cold, hard surface. Everything around him was gray. Both the land and the sky. There were no signs of life.

It made Alden think of something. It was pictures he'd seen in school. They were learning about planets. The moon looked like this.

Some facts ran through his mind. One stood out from the rest. There was no air on the moon. How was he alive right now?

He checked the scores. Mad Dog and Destroyer had all their lives. Cosma had only three.

As Black Heart got to his feet, a rock exploded. Someone had fired from above. He looked up. There was a ship. Cosma was coming right for him.

He started running. A shower of bullets hit the ground

around him. They ripped into the surface. Chunks of rock flew up. In their place were huge holes.

One was a few feet ahead of him. This was his chance. Black Heart ran for it, dodging bullets. Time was running out. He ran faster. Then he pushed off into a leap.

The motion shot him past the hole. He crashed hard into the surface. He'd need another place to hide. But now it was hard to see. The fall had partially blinded him. He scrambled along the ground.

So far Alden hadn't panicked. He wasn't going to quit. But this felt all too real. Game or no game, Black Heart was on the moon. And he couldn't see. He was gasping for air.

Was he Black Heart? Or was he Alden? It seemed like the worlds were becoming one.

Suddenly he felt himself falling. There was no time to brace. His body slammed into the ground.

The fall should have knocked him out. He almost wished it had. The pain was so bad. His arms and legs began to shake. Then everything went dark.

♛

Black Heart opened his eyes. The sky was bright orange. In place of the moon was hot desert sand. Was that a pyramid over there? This looked like Egypt. He tapped the headset for his score.

"Lives used: 2. Lives left: 2."

Mad Dog and Destroyer were standing nearby. It didn't make sense. Were Lee and Dev working together? They had a better chance of winning that way. Then they could split the prize money.

Alden could have done that with Nina. Except it was cheating. He'd do anything to win but that.

There was no time to think. A battle was about to begin. It wouldn't be easy. The sand was heavy and hot. But when Black Heart turned around, there was no sand.

Chapter 8

OFF THE WALL

Dry desert was now dark, damp forest. Plants covered every inch of ground. Trees towered above. They blocked most of the sun. Still, it was warm. This was a rainforest.

Black Heart made his way along the forest floor. It was a maze of tangled vines and thick shrubs. The dim light made it hard to see. Then he remembered the blade. He used it to cut back the brush.

As he took another whack, he saw it. A snake was coiled around a branch. It had the markings of a cobra. It was close enough to touch. The snake raised its head and hissed. It was about to strike.

Of all the enemies he could face. Alden would not lose to a snake. He needed every life he had left.

Thinking fast, Black Heart swung the blade. With one clean slice, the snake's head went flying.

Just then there was a noise. It was loud shrieks. *Just monkeys.* Then there was movement. It was coming from the brush. Mad Dog? Destroyer?

Black Heart began slashing through the forest. Finally he came to a clearing. Just beyond was a hut. He walked up to it and looked inside.

The room was empty. Wait. Something was on the floor. It was a tiny bottle. Black Heart picked it up. Yes! This was part of the cure! He put it into his pocket.

And there was something else. A picture was on the wall. It wasn't hanging straight. He looked more closely. There was writing behind it.

Computer code? This was exciting! The game instructions didn't mention it. But most video games had hidden gems. This could be a way to hack the game. It could mean a sure win.

Whatever it was, he had to remember it. Black Heart looked around for a pencil or something. This was stupid. Then he checked his pocket. There was a phone! He pulled it out and took a picture.

"Cure one of eight found," a voice said. "First piece of code found."

First piece? Alden thought. How many were there? And what was it for?

Black Heart looked around. Before he could blink, the hut exploded. His body was in flames. He'd be dead any second.

"Score!" Alden screamed.

"Lives used: 4. Lives left: 0."

"No! I have one life left!" This was a mistake.

No Place Like It

Get up, Alden," someone called. "It's time for breakfast."

The voice cut through the fog in his brain. But he couldn't tell who it was. His eyes slowly opened. He blinked as he tried to focus.

This was his bedroom. All of his things were here. His computer and several tablets. A collection of action figures. All the Transformer toys. The trophy on his dresser. How did he get here?

Wait. Trophy? He got out of bed to look at it. "Alden Nash. 4th Place. World Quest."

He opened the door and went downstairs. Alden's parents were on the couch reading.

"I called you for breakfast," his mom said. "You said you'd be down. Did you go back to sleep? Now it's late. School already started."

Alden checked the time. It was 11:02. He just stood there. Weird. That was the time he started playing *World Quest*. It was the last thing he remembered before waking up.

"Are you feeling better?" his dad asked. "That game must have been rough. You were really out of it."

"I'm fine. I think," Alden said. "It's just that—"

"What?" his mom said.

"I had one life left. The game wasn't over."

"It's not like you really lost," his dad said. "Think about the money you made."

"But I didn't finish the game."

"You don't remember?" his mom asked. She turned her laptop toward him.

Alden took a step closer and leaned down. There he was in a photo. The *World Quest* trophy was in his hands.

"A car brought you home," she said. "Lia was with you."

Alden shook his head. "No. That's not right. I was in the hut. I found part of the cure and a code. Then the hut exploded. But the game wasn't over. I don't remember getting the trophy. Or having my picture taken."

"Code?" his dad said. "That sounds interesting. What kind of code?"

"Never mind," Alden said. He went to his room to get ready for school.

Alden got to campus. He checked his phone. There were no messages. Not from Lia. Not even his agent. That was odd. They must have been upset that he lost. But why would that matter to Lia?

If Alden really lost the game, that was okay. But he couldn't shake the feeling. Something had gone wrong.

Then a memory flashed in his mind. Alden was in the hut. He saw a code and took a photo. It was just before the explosion.

He opened the camera app on his phone. There it was! But why was it on his own phone? He had used the *World Quest* phone.

The day was about to get stranger.

Kids were talking about the game. It was like Alden wasn't there.

"*World Quest* is awesome!"

"That was an epic game!"

Most of them were talking about his loss.

"Alden Nash sucks."

"Game of shame."

Why was no one talking about the life Alden had left? The one he never played. His friends would know. But none of them were around. He couldn't even find Lia.

"Where R U babe?" he texted.

"Sick 2day," she texted back.

At noon, Alden was leaving campus to get food. The usual guard wasn't there. He knew Alden well. The new guard asked for Alden's ID. He had to show he was a senior.

Alden reached into his back pocket. The ID wasn't there.

"Sorry," the guard said.

"But I always leave for lunch. Mr. Scott knows—"

"I'm on duty today. If you have a problem, see the principal. But you're not leaving campus."

Alden gazed past the guard. He was eyeing the gate. The thought of running went through his mind. But then he turned around. It wasn't worth it. He'd have to wait till after school. Maybe Lia could help him make sense of this.

Chapter 10

GET REAL

There was a car in front of Lia's house. It didn't look familiar. No one in her family had one like it.

Alden pulled in front of the house and parked. He walked up to the door and knocked.

The door opened. It was Lia's mom. "Yes?" she said.

"Hi, Mrs. Bishop."

She just looked at him.

"I'd like to say hi to Lia. Can you let her know I'm here?"

"I don't think that's a good idea. She's very ill. The poor girl can't keep food down."

This didn't sound like Lia's mom. She was usually so friendly.

"I'll be quick," Alden said. He had to talk to Lia. She was the only normal thing in his life right now.

"Okay," Mrs. Bishop said. She stepped aside to let Alden in. Then she closed the door. "Let me tell her you're here." She vanished down the hallway. After a few seconds, she returned. "She'll see you."

His visits to the Bishop house were never this formal. What was going on? He walked down the hallway to Lia's bedroom. Her door was halfway shut, so he knocked.

"Come in," Lia said.

Her voice sounds normal, Alden thought. He walked into her room. She just looked at him.

"You're not happy to see me?" he said.

"I am," Lia said. "But I've been so sick. You shouldn't stay too long."

"You don't look that sick."

Alden thought she looked fine. Even her hair looked nice. Then he noticed how tidy her room was. Normally it was a mess. Books would be scattered everywhere. But not now.

Nothing in the room made Alden think she was sick. There were no tissues. No glass of juice. Not even bottled water.

"Your mom said you're really sick. You can't stop throwing up."

"I guess I'm getting better. Hey, how stoked are you on *World Quest*? You made so much money."

Talk about a sudden change of topic. But he did want to talk to her about it. "The money's good," he said. "But I'm not happy about losing. Especially when I had a life left. And I found a part of the cure. With that piece of code, I could have won!"

"Code? Sounds cool. Can you show me?"

Alden looked at her. Why would she even care? He was getting a bad feeling.

"Never mind," he said. "I'm just bummed about it."

"How come you didn't say something at Grunt Games?"

"That's the problem. I don't remember anything after the explosion. The next thing I knew, I woke up in my room."

"Come on," she said. "I was in the car that picked you up. You should remember. You were wrecked. It was from playing the game too long."

"How do you know that?"

"You told me. That's what the people at Grunt said. The game went on too long. It messed with your mind. And now they're going to make changes."

"Changes?" Alden asked.

"Yeah. To make the game better. Before they sell it. It's going to be huge."

"That still doesn't explain one thing. Why didn't I get to use my last life?"

"Maybe you lost two lives in the explosion. Or maybe Grunt changed the rules. They were still working on the game."

This was not the girl Alden knew. It almost sounded like she'd been programmed.

Chapter 11

Gotta Run

The whole day had been strange. It was like Alden was dreaming. If only he could reboot. Instead, he started his homework. He had a book report due.

He opened his laptop. A notice popped up. It was an email. The sender was "Unknown." The subject line said, "This is not you."

Spam, he thought. He started to delete it. Then there was another email. The sender was the same. But the subject was a little different. "This is not your life."

Someone was trying hard to get his attention. Alden opened the email. It was blank. "What do you want?" he replied.

There was no answer. He left email up in case of another message. But he closed his book report. He wanted to get some gaming in before dinner.

Then his phone buzzed. It was a text. "Trust no one." Another text came in. "You're still in the game."

Alden stared at his phone. His heart was pounding. Who was this? Suddenly he heard a voice. It was coming from downstairs. It wasn't his mom or dad. He went to his door and leaned out.

"I need to speak to your son," the voice said.

"He's upstairs, Officer."

Officer?

"I'll get him," his dad said.

Alden heard footsteps.

"I'll come with you," the voice said.

It sounded like several people were coming.

"He's in his bedroom," his dad said.

How many cops were there? What did they want? And why had his dad allowed this invasion?

Alden quietly shut the door. But now he was cornered. He looked at the window. It was the only way out. With seconds to spare, he grabbed his phone. Then he tossed his heavy backpack in front of the door. That would slow them down.

He opened the window and pushed the screen out. Just below was a deck. It wasn't a long drop. But from there, it was about 15 feet to the ground.

His dad called out. The doorknob turned. Alden

climbed out the window and sat on the ledge. Then he pushed himself off and dropped.

Voices were coming from his room. Now for the jump to the ground. There was one chance to do it right. A bad fall would mean getting hurt. Or worse, caught.

Here goes nothing. Alden landed with a thud. The fall dazed him. *Shake it off! You need to get out of here.*

The email had said to trust no one. But Alden needed help. Somehow his legs carried him to Lia's street. Lights were flashing. There were cop cars in front of her house. Two cops were standing guard.

Alden watched from behind some bushes. He could hear the crackle of a police radio. A voice said his name. Cops were looking for him. Why?

This wasn't right. Alden Nash was not a criminal.

BLUR

Alden looked out from the bushes. A beam of light hit his eyes. A cop was holding a flashlight. He headed Alden's way then stopped. It was like he'd seen something. But he turned and walked away.

Now the beam hit a car's bumper. Alden saw numbers. They looked like the code he'd found in *World Quest*. He wasn't taking chances. He took a picture with his phone.

"Second piece of code found," a voice said.

Just then there was a strong wind. A loud noise filled the sky.

Whop, *whop*, *whop*.

It was the blades of a helicopter. It was over Alden's head. A bright ring of light beamed down on him.

"Alden Nash!" a voice shouted over a microphone. The sound echoed through the street.

Run! he told himself. But he stood there frozen. He wondered if Lia could see him.

"Get down on the ground!"

Part of Alden wanted this to end. Instead, he took a few steps. It was like someone had control of him. Signals were being sent to his legs. He took off in a sprint.

"Get him!" a voice yelled.

Cops got into their cars and sped off. Sirens were blaring. The helicopter followed.

Alden knew this area well. There was an alley nearby. It led to a park where he could hide.

Now the sirens were getting closer. Alden turned into the alley. He was almost to the end. Just a few more—

His pace slowed. "What the—" Something wasn't right. The alley ended ahead. There was a brick wall. Footsteps were coming up fast from behind. The helicopter was following.

"Freeze! Or we'll shoot!" a cop shouted.

Alden stood there. He was trapped. Slowly he turned around. Several rifles were aimed his way. He took a step back.

"I said don't move!" the cop yelled.

Suddenly there was a loud noise. It was bricks crumbling. Pieces fell to the ground. Alden felt someone grab him from behind. A muscular arm had him by the waist.

"Hey!" he called. All at once, he flew backward.

Whoosh! He was through the wall.

Alden couldn't see a face. Just a shiny bald head and bulging muscles.

"Who are you?" Alden asked.

Now the cops were firing.

"No time for questions!" the man said as he shot back. Regular guns were no match for his weapon. "Follow me!"

Where they were going wasn't clear. But the stranger seemed to have a plan. Soon they were in the backyard of a home.

The man ripped the back door from its frame. Alden followed him inside. There was nothing there. The house was empty.

Suddenly shots rang out. The cops were firing again. Glass shattered as they blew out the windows.

"Keep up!" the stranger called to Alden. He went to the front door and opened it. Just as the cops entered, he pushed Alden outside. A black Hummer was waiting on the street.

"Let's go!" the man said. He ran to the Hummer and jumped in.

Alden stopped to look around. The houses were all the same. They were plain gray boxes. There were no windows.

He ran to the Hummer and got in.

Chapter 13

MASTERMIND

"What's going on?" Alden asked. "You're scaring me."

Now Alden could see the man's face. Besides a bald head, he had a goatee. There was a tattoo on his neck. His eyes were dark. But there was also something kind about them.

"Why so nervous?" the man asked. "That's not the wise guy I know." He gunned the engine.

Alden was barely inside when the man swung a U-turn. The motion sent Alden flying. He nearly fell out. Tires screeched as the Hummer peeled away.

Cop cars were coming. As Alden closed the door, he looked back. They'd left the cops in a cloud of smoke.

"Who are you?" Alden asked.

"Mastermind," he said.

That sounded familiar. "A gaming character?"

"Yes. It's what some gaming critics call me."

"You mean—"

"It's me, Alden. Andrew Foster."

Alden looked closely at the avatar. "No way! From Grunt Games?"

"For now at least."

"What do you mean?"

"They want to fire me."

It didn't make sense. Foster was a genius. Grunt would be nothing without him.

"I'll try to explain," Foster said. "Grunt wanted to get into VR."

"Right. That's *World Quest*. It's awesome."

"It *was* awesome. Look. We don't have much time. I'll get to the point. The real goal is mind control."

"I don't understand," Alden said.

"I created *World Quest*. Then my bosses wanted a second world. It's called *Alpha X*. It looks like a player's own world. They'd face the same type of challenges. But with people in their lives."

"That sounds cool."

"I liked the idea too," Foster said.

"So what's the problem?" Alden asked.

"It's what Grunt wanted to do next. People would finish playing *World Quest*. They'd take off the headset.

But the game wasn't over. Players would be in *Alpha X*. Then Grunt could program them. Make them do things. Put thoughts in their heads. You're in *Alpha X* now."

Alden nodded. "That's why nothing's been quite right."

"They found out about your life. Then they copied it in game form."

"It's a pretty bad copy," Alden said.

Chapter 14

Control Yourself

I still don't get it," Alden said. "What does Grunt want?"

"Right now, they're after you. They know you have two pieces of code. When you get the last piece, they can control you."

"How? Why?"

"I told you," Foster said. "*Alpha X* has a mind control feature."

"Okay. But you made it. Were you in on the plan?" Alden asked.

"Never," Foster said. "It was meant to be fun for players. First of all, they would know about it. Then they could choose. To play as themselves. Or they could give up control. The game would tell them what to do."

"And then?" Alden said.

"Grunt wanted to keep the code secret. Players wouldn't know they'd lost control. I couldn't let that happen. So I split the code into pieces. Then I hid them in the game."

"But you're Andrew Foster. It's your game. Just take the code out."

"That was my plan," Foster said. "But time ran out. They found out I'm against them. Now they watch every move I make. I was lucky to get this time with you. Everyone left for lunch. I locked the door. I'm coding myself into the game."

"This can't be real," Alden said. "Controlling people's minds?"

"It's more real than you know. And *Alpha X* is just the start. That's why I have to stop this now."

"What's the contest for?"

"I wanted *World Quest* to be completed. Then it could be sold. My bosses agreed to a contest. It would get a lot of hype. More money could be made. They don't know the real reason."

"What is it?"

"I can't touch the code," Foster said. "But players can. I built the game that way. Once a player finds all the pieces, I can hack in and grab it. My bosses will never know."

Alden was still confused.

"This might make you feel better," Foster said. "You weren't picked at random. I asked for you."

"Really?"

"I'm a big fan. You're a great gamer, Alden. You're also smart. I knew you would find the code. And that you would help me."

"How would you know that? Maybe I don't want to."

"That's not Alden Nash. He doesn't have a black heart. He fights for good causes, not evil."

This all sounded so creepy. It's like he knew Alden from his gaming habits. Or his thoughts. "Where am I now?" Alden asked. "I mean the real me."

"You're at Grunt," Foster said. "Sitting in the gaming room. They know you've found the two pieces of code. They're just waiting for you to find the third. Then they'll mess with your mind."

"What about people watching the game. What do they think happened?"

"That you were killed."

"But I still had a life left," Alden said.

"Doesn't matter. All Grunt cares about is using the code."

"Do they plan to kill me? I mean *really* kill me."

"No," Foster said. "You're just an experiment. You'll be allowed to go. But they'll watch you. In case you remember things they did. But let's not think about that. We will get the code."

"Do they know you're here? I mean that Mastermind is here?"

"They might by now. I told them I wanted to play."

"How do we find the last piece of code?"

Just then there was a flood of bright lights. Dozens of cop cars were on their tail. There were tanks too. Helicopters followed.

"The big bad bots are coming. Let's have some fun," Foster said.

CODE OH NO

Can I call you by your real name?" Alden asked. "Mastermind seems a little formal."

"Sure."

Now Foster was weaving in and out of traffic. Along the way, cars swerved and crashed.

"How fast are we going?" Alden asked.

"Don't know. There's no gauge on this thing."

He made a hard right onto a narrow road. Cop cars soon followed. Their sirens were screaming.

Ahead of the Hummer was a line of tanks. They moved steadily closer. But Foster didn't slow down. Instead, he stepped on the gas.

Alden looked off to the side. There was a steep cliff. This wasn't going to end well.

"Hold on," Foster said.

Just before hitting the first tank, he swerved. The car from behind hit the tank head on. There were a string of crashes. Cars spun out. Some flew off the cliff. Then gas tanks blew up and burst into flames.

Bullets rained down from the helicopters. The Hummer was filled with holes.

"Let's go!" Foster said. He jumped out of the speeding Hummer.

Alden followed him. They ran into some bushes.

"Stay low!" Foster called. "I don't want to fight. That'll just delay getting the code. And Grunt could take over the game."

Bullets kept flying. A minute went by. Then everything got quiet. The cops and helicopters were gone. By now it was dark.

"Come on," Foster said.

They started walking down the road. In a few miles, they came to some buildings. The windows were shattered. Some buildings had been blown up. Only piles of rubble were left.

Then the sirens started up. Cop cars and tanks swarmed in. The helicopters were back too. Bullets flew.

"Is the code here?" Alden asked.

"Hold on," Foster said. The cops and tanks began to vanish. Then the helicopters faded away. "I'm recoding the scene."

"Why did you wait so long? Code us the heck out of here!"

"There's still something we need. Remember? The third piece of mind control code. Look! There it is!" Foster was pointing at the ground.

"Should I take a picture of it?" Alden asked.

"I've got it," Foster said. "But give me your phone."

Foster inserted a memory card. He copied Alden's two photos of the code. "Now I'm going to delete these," he said. "In case they check when you're back at Grunt."

"You have what you need," Alden said. "Can we get out of here now?"

"No."

"What? But you said—"

"You need to finish the game."

"Wait," Alden said. "What are you doing?"

"Sending you back."

"To *World Quest*?"

"You have to use your last life. I want you to win this."

"But where will—"

"I'll help you if I can. My bosses are at the door. See you soon."

Game On

Black Heart was back in the game! He checked his weapons. All were there. What about the bottle of the cure he'd found? It was only one of eight. But it was better than none. And without it, there was no chance to win. *Yes!* The bottle was in his pocket.

Now he looked around the room. It was dark gray. Panels of blinking lights lined one wall. The view from a window showed deep space. This room was in a spaceship.

On another wall was a screen. An image popped up. It was Mad Dog. Over his picture were the words "Lives Left: 0." Lee was out of the game. It was the same for Destroyer. Dev was out too.

Then the screen went dark. That meant one thing.

Nina was still playing. Her avatar would show up any time.

"I've been waiting for you," a voice said.

Black Heart didn't move. He knew it was Cosma. She was holding a gun to his head.

"You're all that's left in my way." She pressed harder into his head. "Time for you to leave this game for good. But first things first. Hand over the bottle."

Just then something hit the ship. The force sent them flying. They slammed into a wall and fell.

Cosma looked stunned. Her gun was on the floor. This was Black Heart's only chance. He had to get it away from her. As he got to his feet, the ship was struck again.

Black Heart fell. A gun went off. Blood was coming from his shoulder. Cosma had shot him. Now she stood over him, looking down. He didn't have time to pull a weapon. This was the end.

Another shot rang out. Then all got quiet. A hole had been fired into Cosma's head. She slumped to the floor.

Black Heart stood up. He looked down at Cosma. She'd almost won this game. Then he looked around. Someone had saved him.

He checked the pocket of her jacket. The bottles were there. He took them out and counted. There were seven. He pulled his bottle out of his pocket. That made eight.

Black Heart had the cure. He could save the world. The only goal now was to get back to home base.

An image came up on the screen. It was Cosma. Over that were the words "Lives Left: 0."

The control panel lit up. There was a message. The ship had been hit. Pieces of space junk had rammed it.

A red light flashed. It was a warning. More junk was coming. A screen showed the ship. It bounced with each hit. It looked like a game of pinball.

If only it were that easy. But using thoughts to control Black Heart was no longer working. The avatar sat still at the control panel. That's when Alden felt something beneath his fingertips. A keyboard! Alden was in control now.

One hand started tapping keys. The other reached for the mouse. The ship went into hyperdrive. Debris flew at it like bullets. Alden moved the ship with precision. It dodged every piece of junk. Foster had to be seeing this right now. He'd be proud.

Boom!

A large rock had slammed into the ship. It ripped a hole in the fuel tank. Fuel was running out fast. Making it to Earth would be impossible. But Alden was in win mode. He had to try.

Then a code popped up on the control panel. Alden

typed it in. The fuel supply was restored. Was Foster helping him? He'd said he would if he could.

"Let's get this done!" Alden said.

His fingers kept tapping keys. The ship fell through space. Pieces broke off. They looked like big balls of light.

Alden's life was on the line. Wait! No it wasn't. This was a game. The thought calmed him. But he still wanted to win.

First he had to get back to Earth. He fired the engines. The ship slowed down. Next there would be intense heat. But the ship's heat shield was damaged. Tiles had been ripped away. Were there enough to survive? He was about to find out.

A message came up on the control panel. The computer was taking over. It would land the ship. It began to shake. Alden felt the heat. Flames came up around the ship.

From the window, he saw Earth. It was a ball of swirling blues and white. The sight put him in a daze.

He thought back over this adventure. Playing *World Quest* was awesome. He'd even been able to help Foster.

Then Alden thought about his life. He'd lived it playing games. They were better than the real world. Now he felt differently. He couldn't wait to get home. No amount of money could replace it.

The ship had withstood reentry. It was flying smoothly like a plane. Control was back with Alden. He began to direct Black Heart with his thoughts.

Line up the plane with the landing strip. Make the approach. Lower the landing gear. Touch down. Bring the plane to a stop.

Alden checked his score.

"Win!"

Chapter 17

Over and Out

Nice job!" a voice said.

Alden could feel the person touching him. They took something off his head. For a second he didn't know where he was.

Slowly he started to focus. Alden was sitting in a chair. This was where he'd been playing *World Quest*.

"We all thought Cosma had you."

Alden looked up at her. She was holding his headset.

"Do you know who I am?"

He nodded. It was Lana Wong, the woman who had first greeted him. She pointed to the screen on the wall. Photos of Nina, Dev, and Lee came up. Nina had won second place. Dev and Lee tied for third.

Then the scene changed. Crowds of people filled the

screen. A banner ran across the bottom. It repeated the same phrase over and over.

"Alden Nash—Winner of *World Quest!*"

People waved. It looked like they were shouting. Lana turned on the sound. A roar of cheers filled the room. People clapped. Some chanted. "Black Heart! Black Heart!"

"Can they see me?" he asked.

"Yes."

Alden waved. People went crazy.

"The contest was a success," Lana said.

"What time is it?" Alden asked.

"It's 3:02. You played exactly four hours."

It felt like a year, Alden thought.

A door opened. Men and women entered the room. They stood around Alden. Some shook his hand. Others thanked him.

Alden scanned the faces. Was Foster here? Then he thought about *Alpha X*. Were these the bosses Foster spoke of? Did they know about the code? That he tried to take it out of the game? It didn't seem like it. They were all so happy.

One of the men held a trophy. He handed it to Alden.

"Alden Nash," he said. "You are the world's number one gamer. No one has more fans than you do. Your numbers on social media prove it. *World Quest* is going to sell like crazy."

A woman stepped forward. She handed him an envelope. "You've more than earned this."

Alden took it from her.

"It's a check for one million dollars," she said.

Cheers erupted from the crowd. But Alden barely heard them. He still had questions. Had Foster been fired? Did he take the mind control code out of *Alpha X*?

Alden felt dizzy. All the noise was too much. He had to get out of there.

He stood up. "Thanks. It was fun."

Lana walked him to the door. Before leaving, he turned to look back. The group just stared at him. For a second he wondered if he was still in the game. Maybe they'd taken over his brain.

Alden went through the scanner. The guard gave him his phone and keys. Then he left the building.

Chapter 18

VIRTUAL REALITY BITES

After being stuck inside, the fresh air felt good. Then Alden saw Lia. She had a big smile on her face. Seeing her was better than playing any game. It was even better than having a million bucks.

"You did it," Lia said. "I'm so proud of you."

Alden hurried over and hugged her. He didn't want to let go. So much had happened in the game. It changed him somehow. He'd always cared for Lia. But now he knew the value of what they had.

"Let's go," she said. "The car's waiting."

On the drive home, Alden stared out the window. He was quiet the whole time. It was the mind control that worried him. How far had Grunt gone?

Were they messing with his mind now? They could be following him. He turned to look out the back window.

Maybe they were programming Lia. She could be out to get him. He looked over at her.

Was this how life would be? Playing *World Quest* hadn't been worth it. The money wasn't worth it. Alden wanted to talk to Lia. But he knew how it would sound. She'd think he was crazy.

Right now he just wanted to talk to Foster.

Alden's phone went off. It was his agent.

"Answer it," Lia said.

"Nah," he said. "I don't want to talk to anyone."

"Come on. Don't be such a baby. It might be your parents."

"It's just Zac. I don't want to talk business."

"But it might be a deal," Lia said.

That's what Alden was afraid of. He wanted a break from gaming. His phone buzzed. Zac had sent a text.

"Congrats, man! Big deals in the works. $$$. Call me."

Alden called Zac. "I want to take a few weeks off," he said.

"Are you serious?" Zac asked. "You're on fire. Take advantage while you can."

"It's not forever," Alden said. "I'll let you know when I'm ready." He ended the call.

"Are you okay?" Lia asked. "Did something happen to you in that game?"

Lia really did care about him. It would be so easy to tell her everything. She would have listened. And it would have made him feel better. But something stopped him. For now it would be his secret.

"Not really," Alden said. "There's just more to life than gaming."

He saw Lia glance over at him. She looked confused. Alden knew what she was thinking. For him to say there was more than gaming? Something must have happened.

Chapter 19

The Real Deal

It had been a week since the *World Quest* game. Alden needed that time to get back to normal.

For the first few days, he looked for signs. Were people looking at him funny? Was he being followed? Had he done anything he wouldn't normally do? Punch someone? Crash a car?

He watched his parents. They seemed to be normal. They spent a lot of time fussing over him. His mom made all his favorite meals. And his dad wanted to know about upcoming deals. That was his dad for sure. It was all about the money.

Alden even went over to see Lia's mom. He wanted to make sure Mrs. Bishop was really herself. She was. She gave him a big hug.

Finally he was convinced. No one was controlling his mind.

Now he was walking through the halls of Volt High. Kids called out as he went by.

"Epic plays, man!"

"You crushed it!"

"How's it feel to be a millionaire?"

"Nash is rolling in cash!"

Alden smiled and waved to his fans. "Thanks, guys! Your support means a lot."

"How does it feel to be so loved?" Lia asked. She'd come up behind him. They were meeting to go get lunch.

"By my fans? Or by you?" he said smiling.

"I have to admit. I wasn't a huge fan of Black Heart. But I love the new Alden Nash."

"How am I new?" Alden asked.

"You seem more humble."

Alden shrugged. "I guess I've learned a few things."

"Oh yeah? What?" Lia asked.

He acted like he was thinking. "Well … I was right about PC players. We rule!"

"Oh, you! Can't you ever be serious?" But Lia was laughing. She'd always loved Alden's sense of humor.

They came up to the school gate. The campus guard was there to check IDs. Alden didn't have his. He got nervous for a second. Would the man try to stop him?

The guard looked at Lia. Then he looked at Alden. "Alden Nash," he said.

"Yeah," Alden said.

"We're all so proud of you. Would you sign this for me?" He held out a small notepad. "I love to—I mean my kids love to watch you play."

Alden smiled. "You got it."

♕

It was a few weeks later. Things were good. Alden and Lia had been spending time together. Life wasn't just about games.

But there was this one new game. It was called *Slate*. Alden had gotten good at it.

Slate was nothing like *World Quest*. It didn't have all the drama. But the story was good. There were a lot of relationships. It got personal. And there were puzzles to solve. It was real-life stuff. Alden liked that.

He told his agent he'd like to compete. Then he got a deal. He'd been practicing a little each day. But today he took a break.

He and Lia were hanging out at his house. They were sitting on the couch. Lia was on her laptop. Alden had his eyes closed. His head was on her shoulder.

"Look at this, babe." Lia was reading a story. It was on a gaming site. "It's about Grunt Games."

Alden sat up. He listened as she read parts of it.

"*World Quest* is on hold. It won't be coming out this year. Changes are needed. Some parts of the game didn't work right."

Alpha X, Alden thought.

"Grunt Games was sold," Lia read. "Another big company bought it. It's called Reckless. The whole Grunt staff was fired."

"Is there anything about Andrew Foster?"

"Yeah," Lia said. "Reckless kept him. He's working on *World Quest*. Didn't you meet him?"

Alden shook his head. "Not really."

"And listen to this. That new game you've been playing? *Slate*? He created it."

"No way!"

GREAT MINDS

Foster had brought Grunt Games down. He must have gotten the mind control code. This was great news. He'd love to talk to the man. He still hadn't met him. Not in person anyway. And now Alden was playing Foster's new game. This was amazing.

Just then Alden's phone buzzed. He looked at the name on the screen. Mastermind. He felt a chill go through him. Could he still be in *World Quest*?

"Who is it?" Lia asked.

"I'm not sure," Alden said. If it really was Foster, that would be awesome. Then he read the text.

"Am in the area. Would like to meet. Coffee in 20 minutes? The place on the corner."

"Sure," Alden texted back. He looked at Lia. "It's Andrew Foster."

"The guy I was just reading about?"

He nodded. How did Foster know where to find him? These big gaming guys seemed to know everything. Alden had been playing Foster's new game. Maybe he'd been tracking him somehow.

"What does he want?" Lia asked.

"To meet with me."

"Why aren't you smiling? You should be excited right now. This was your dream. To meet Andrew Foster."

"Yeah, I know." He looked at Lia. "About *World Quest*," he started. "I haven't told you everything."

"So something *did* happen to you?"

"I kind of lost my mind," he said. "I never want to feel like that again."

Lia didn't say anything. Instead, she put her arms around him. She knew him well. He would talk when he was ready.

♕

It was a warm, sunny day. Alden and Lia walked to the corner. The parking lot of the coffee place was packed. Alden did a quick scan of the cars. No Hummers.

He opened the door for Lia. She stepped inside. As he went in, he looked around. How would he know Foster? Would he look like Mastermind? Bald head. Goatee.

The place was crowded. But something caught his eye. It was a man with a bald head. His back was to them.

"Over there," Alden said to Lia. "I think that's him." He headed toward the table. Lia followed.

The man suddenly turned around. It *was* him! Foster was Mastermind! He stood up.

"Alden!" he called. "It is so nice to see you." He reached out. The two shook hands.

"This is my girlfriend, Lia," Alden said.

"Hi, Lia. Before we talk, do you want to order?"

Alden looked at Lia. She shook her head. "We're fine right now," Alden said. "Um. I'm just wondering. Where's your tattoo? The one you had on your neck."

Foster laughed. "You mean the skull? That was just for the game. I wanted to look tough. It was a lot of fun."

"So ..." Alden started to say.

"I know. You want some answers. Grunt Games is done. There will be no mind control. At least not the kind that can hurt people. I'm working at Reckless now. They give me all the creative freedom I've ever wanted. I can make the games I've dreamed about. And I'd like you to join me, Alden."

"Wow," Alden said. "That's ... that's—"

"Amazing is what he means," Lia said.

Foster laughed.

"Sorry," Alden said. "I'm just surprised."

"Are you kidding?" Foster said. "Think about how we worked together in *World Quest*. And we had fun doing it!"

"Yeah, fun. But—"

"I know what you're thinking," Foster said. "You don't want to play games like *World Quest*. I understand. But you've been playing *Slate*. I've seen your online scores. You really get it. The whole personal journey experience."

"It's amazing," Alden said. "I've never played anything like it. The adventures are awesome. And the puzzles are fun. But they teach lessons. I never thought I'd like that kind of stuff. But it gets into your brain."

"Well, I did create it with you in mind. So here's my offer. When you graduate, you've got a job at Reckless. You'll be in charge of development. What do you say?"

"No more shooter games," Alden said. "And I'd like to start a division. I want to mentor young gamers."

"I love it," Foster said. "Mastermind and the Mentor. So we have a deal?"

Alden looked at Lia. "One more thing," he said. "I'll need nights and weekends off."

"Done! Now, can I drive you home?"

"Sure," Alden said.

They got up from the table and went outside.

"My car is over here," Foster said.

Alden and Lia followed him. They turned the corner. That's when Alden saw it. The Hummer was parked there. He stopped. Foster looked back.

"Um, you know what," Alden said. "It's such a nice day. I think we'll walk."

Foster smiled. "I'll call you soon."

WANT TO KEEP READING?

9781680214772

Turn the page for a sneak peek
at another book in the Monarch
Jungle series.

Chapter 1

BEING KEVIN SANDERS

Kevin Sanders!" people shouted. "I love your videos!"

"Make sure to like and comment," Kevin said. He pushed his hair back and smiled.

Fans held up their phones. He posed for photos.

"Let's go," a man said. He was Kevin's helper. Right now he had one job. Get the star through the crowd.

A path had been roped off. But some fans ducked under it.

"Back!" the man yelled.

"Pipeline," Kevin called. "Come to the booth." He held up his phone. Fans cheered.

Hollywood had film stars. These were online stars. There were dancers and singers. Some wrote books. Others were bloggers. Many stars gave tips. They were about fashion and makeup.

Their posts got millions of views. It was how regular people got famous. There was a name for it. Instafamous.

Take Kevin. He did pranks. Millions loved his YouTube videos. When he wasn't posting, he was at events. Meeting fans was important.

Today he was at See It Live. It was held once a year in LA. Tickets sold out in minutes. If you were here, you'd made it.

Fans were a big part. But it was also about business. Agents handled that. They made deals. Companies paid stars to use their products. That was how Kevin teamed up with Pipeline Clothing.

They saw a video he made. He was surfing with a shark. Then the video went viral. The company wanted a deal. Three million people followed Kevin on Instagram. One photo of him sold tons of stuff. In this case, it was surf gear.

Kevin made money too. He got four grand to be here. His agent set it up. Ron Simon made great deals. Today the deal was simple. Wear the clothes and pose for selfies.

"Kevin Sanders!" a woman called out. She was a reporter. "What are you working on?"

"Aww. You know I can't say." He gave her a sly grin. "It'll ruin the surprise."

He was working on a show for YouTube. It was called "I Am Kevin Sanders."

"Come on, Kev," she said. "Tell us."

"Yeah, Kev," a voice said. "We want to know."

It was Chase Rogers. He was also an online star. Sometimes the two teamed up for pranks.

"What's up?" Kevin said.

"Your shirt," Chase said.

"What about it?"

"It's Pipeline's. They hired me! You're a cheap fake!"

"Don't make me hurt you," Kevin said. He gave Chase a push. Suddenly the crowd rushed in. They started to pull the guys apart. But the two had stepped aside. People hadn't seen them. Now the crowd turned on each other.

Kevin headed for the exit. At the door, he looked back. A fight had broken out. Chase was close behind. They each ran to a limo and got in. Kevin called Chase.

"That was epic!" Kevin said.

"Dude!" Chase said. "Check out YouTube. This thing is blowing up! The traffic's on fire!"

"Doesn't take much, does it?"

"Are you kidding? We started a riot."